MW01129384

ANIMALS ON THE FARM

COWS

by Kari Schuetz

BLASTOFF! READERS

BELLWETHER MEDIA · MINNEAPOLIS, MN

Note to Librarians, Teachers, and Parents:

Blastoff! Readers are carefully developed by literacy experts and combine standards-based content with developmentally appropriate text.

Level 1 provides the most support through repetition of high-frequency words, light text, predictable sentence patterns, and strong visual support.

Level 2 offers early readers a bit more challenge through varied simple sentences, increased text load, and less repetition of high-frequency words.

Level 3 advances early-fluent readers toward fluency through increased text and concept load, less reliance on visuals, longer sentences, and more literary language.

Level 4 builds reading stamina by providing more text per page, increased use of punctuation, greater variation in sentence patterns, and increasingly challenging vocabulary.

Level 5 encourages children to move from "learning to read" to "reading to learn" by providing even more text, varied writing styles, and less familiar topics.

Whichever book is right for your reader, Blastoff! Readers are the perfect books to build confidence and encourage a love of reading that will last a lifetime!

This edition first published in 2018 by Bellwether Media, Inc.

No part of this publication may be reproduced in whole or in part without written permission of the publisher. For information regarding permission, write to Bellwether Media, Inc., Attention: Permissions Department, 5357 Penn Avenue South, Minneapolis, MN 55419.

Library of Congress Cataloging-in-Publication Data

Names: Schuetz, Kari, author.
Title: Cows / by Kari Schuetz.
Description: Minneapolis, MN : Bellwether Media, Inc., 2018. | Series:
   Blastoff! Readers. Animals on the Farm | Includes bibliographical
   references and index. | Audience: Ages 5 to 8. | Audience: K to Grade 3.
Identifiers: LCCN 2017029535 | ISBN 9781626177215 (hardcover : alk. paper) | ISBN 9781681035017 (ebook)
Subjects: LCSH: Cows–Juvenile literature.
Classification: LCC SF197.5 S378 2018 | DDC 636.2–dc23
LC record available at https://lccn.loc.gov/2017029535

Text copyright © 2018 by Bellwether Media, Inc. BLASTOFF! READERS and associated logos are trademarks and/or registered trademarks of Bellwether Media, Inc. SCHOLASTIC, CHILDREN'S PRESS, and associated logos are trademarks and/or registered trademarks of Scholastic Inc., 557 Broadway, New York, NY 10012.

Editor: Rebecca Sabelko   Designer: Lois Stanfield

Printed in the United States of America, North Mankato, MN.

Table of Contents

Milking Time!   4

What Are Cows?   8

Life on the Farm   16

Glossary   22

To Learn More   23

Index   24

Milking Time!

A farmer milks
a female cow.
The milk falls
into a bucket.

The cow gives a lot of milk. This can make a bucket of ice cream!

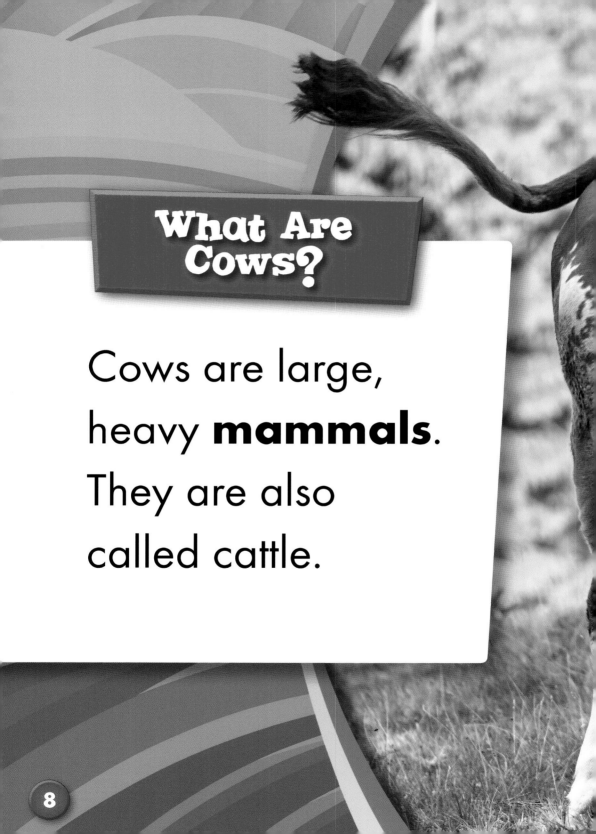

What Are Cows?

Cows are large, heavy **mammals**. They are also called cattle.

NAMES:

males:	bulls
females:	cows
babies:	calves

Hard **split hooves** cover a cow's feet. Each hoof has two toes.

split
hooves

A long, thin tail swats bugs away from a cow's body.

tail

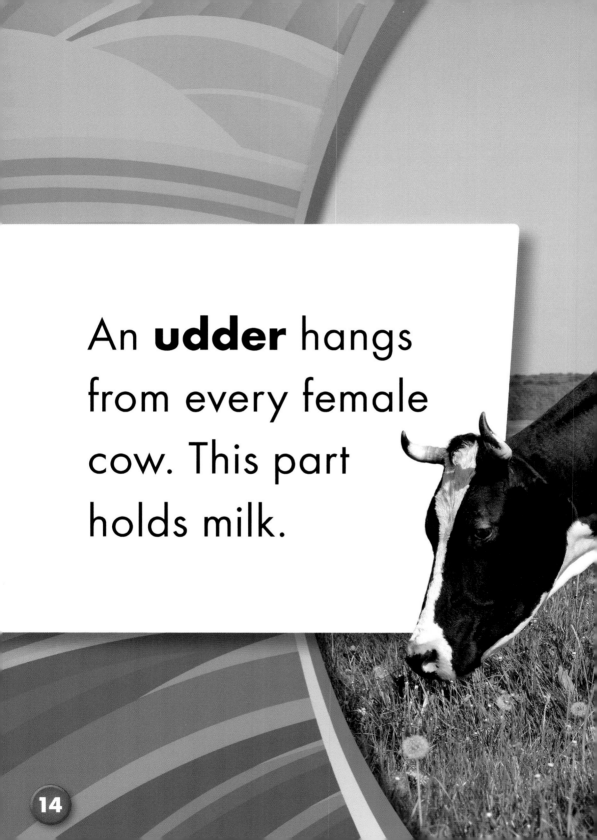

An **udder** hangs from every female cow. This part holds milk.

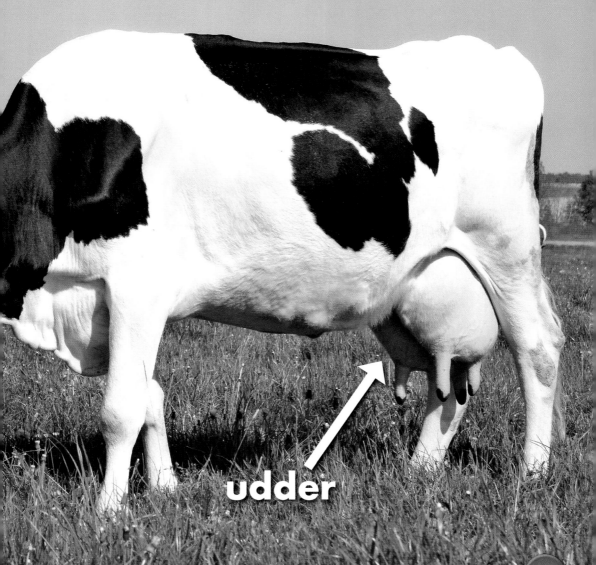

udder

Life on the Farm

Cows move around grassy **pastures** to **graze**. They munch on hay inside barns.

FAVORITE FOODS:
hay, grass, grains

hay

Grass and other food become **cud**. This is food cows spit up and eat again.

Sometimes hungry
cows moo loudly
for food. Time
to eat!

21

Glossary

cud

food that is chewed again after being in the belly

pastures

large fields where cows can feed on grasses

graze

to feed on grasses in a field

split hooves

hard foot coverings that are divided into two parts

mammals

warm-blooded animals that have hair and feed their young milk

udder

the hanging part on a female cow that holds milk

To Learn More

AT THE LIBRARY

Mattern, Joanne. *Farm Animals*. Washington, D.C.: National Geographic, 2017.

Mayerling, Tim. *Calves*. Minneapolis, Minn.: Jump!, 2017.

Pendergast, George. *At the Dairy Farm*. New York, N.Y.: Gareth Stevens Publishing, 2017.

ON THE WEB

Learning more about cows is as easy as 1, 2, 3.

1. Go to www.factsurfer.com.

2. Enter "cows" into the search box.

3. Click the "Surf" button and you will see a list of related web sites.

With factsurfer.com, finding more information is just a click away.

Index

barns, 16
body, 12
bugs, 12
cattle, 8
cud, 18
farmer, 4
feet, 10
females, 4, 9, 14
food, 17, 18, 20
grass, 16, 17, 18
graze, 16
hay, 16, 17
ice cream, 6
mammals, 8
milk, 4, 6, 14
moo, 20, 21

names, 9
pastures, 16
spit, 18
split hooves, 10, 11
swats, 12
tail, 12, 13
toes, 10
udder, 14, 15